W9-BIX-218

Take a Walk, Johnny

by Margaret Hillert
Illustrated by Yoshi Miyake

DEAR CAREGIVER, The *Beginning-to-Read* series is a carefully written collection of classic readers you may remember from your own childhood. Each book features text comprised of common sight words to provide your child ample practice reading the words that appear most frequently in written text. The many additional details in the pictures enhance the story and offer the opportunity for you to help your child expand oral language and develop comprehension.

Begin by reading the story to your child, followed by letting him or her read familiar words and soon your child will be able to read the story independently. At each step of the way, be sure to praise your reader's efforts to build his or her confidence as an independent reader. Discuss the pictures and encourage your child to make connections between the story and his or her own life. At the end of the story, you will find reading activities and a word list that will help your child practice and strengthen beginning reading skills.

Above all, the most important part of the reading experience is to have fun and enjoy it!

Shannon Cannon

Shannon Cannon,
Literacy Consultant

Norwood House Press • P.O. Box 316598 • Chicago, Illinois 60631
For more information about Norwood House Press please visit our website at
www.norwoodhousepress.com or call 866-565-2900.

LIBRARY OF CONGRESS CATALOGING-IN-PUBLICATION DATA
  Hillert, Margaret.
    Take a walk, Johnny / Margaret Hillert ; illustrated by Yoshi Miyake. —
  Rev. and expanded library ed.
      p. cm. — (Beginning-to-read series)
    Summary: "Johnny's summer morning walks, taken initially from boredom,
  become quite adventurous"—Provided by publisher.
    ISBN-13: 978-1-59953-152-6 (library edition : alk. paper)
    ISBN-10: 1-59953-152-6 (library edition : alk. paper) [1.
  Walking—Fiction.] I. Miyake, Yoshi, ill. II. Title.
  PZ7.H558Tak 2008
  [E]—dc22   2007035269

Beginning-to-Read series (c) 2009 by Margaret Hillert.
Library edition published by permission of Pearson Education, Inc. in
arrangement with Norwood House Press, Inc. All rights reserved.
This book was originally published by Follett Publishing Company in 1981.

During the school year Johnny got up early
every morning. He ate a good breakfast
and got dressed. Then he made his bed,
cleaned up his room, and went off to
school with his friends.

When summer came, school was out. Johnny got up early on the first day of summer. He ate a good breakfast and got dressed. Then he made his bed, cleaned up his room, and looked for something to do.

First Johnny played with his toy cars. Then he made silly faces in the mirror and laughed to see himself.

Next Johnny looked at the plants that were growing in the glass box on the table.

After that he went to his mother and said, "Mother, what can I do now? I don't have anything to do."

Mother said, "Take a walk, Johnny."

So Johnny went out to the yard and walked around. He saw a bird up in a tree. He saw a butterfly on a flower. Then, under the flowers, he saw a big, brown toad.

"Hello, toad!" said Johnny. "What a good find you are! You have lots of bumps and funny eyes. Don't jump away, toad. I want to take you into the house and show you to Mother. She'll be surprised!"

Johnny went into the house. "Mother, look at this toad!" he said. "Isn't he great?"

"Yes," said Mother. "He's a fine-looking toad. Why don't you put him into your glass box with the plants? That would be a good place for him."

The next morning Johnny made his bed, cleaned up his room, and looked for something to do.

First he fed the toad. Then he took the toad out of the box and let him hop around the room.

After that Johnny went to his mother and said, "Mother, what can I do now? I don't have anything to do."

Mother said, "Take a walk, Johnny."

Johnny went out to the yard with his toad.
He put the toad back under the flowers.

"Goodbye, toad," said Johnny. "You'll be happier here."

Johnny walked down the sidewalk and looked all around. "I wonder what I'll find today," he said.

Then, under a tree, he saw a rock.

"What a pretty rock," said Johnny. "It has red and white spots, and it even seems to shine a little. I'll take it home and put it with my other rocks."

Johnny went back to his house. "Mother, look at this rock!" he said.

"It's a beautiful rock," said Mother. "I'm glad you found it. You can put it with your other rocks."

The next morning Johnny made his bed, cleaned up his room, and looked for something to do.

First he took out all his rocks. Then he put them all back in boxes again.

After that Johnny went to his mother and said, "Mother, what can I do now? I don't have anything to do."

Mother said, "Take a walk, Johnny."

Johnny went outside. "Take a walk. Take a walk," he said. "That's all I ever seem to do. But this time I know where I'll go."

Johnny walked to the library.

"Just look at all the books," he said. "I can get a book about almost anything. There are books about cowboys and wagons, bridges and mountains, and elephants and circuses. What a wonderful place this is!"

Johnny picked out some books and took them home. "Look here, Mother," he said. "I like to read, and these books are full of good things to read about."

"I see you went to the library," said Mother. "What a good idea! Books are fun to read, and it looks like you found some good ones."

The next morning Johnny made his bed, cleaned up his room, and looked for something to do.

He read for a time. Then he put all his books away.

After that Johnny went to his mother and said, "Mother, what can I do now? I don't have anything to do."

Mother said, "Take a walk, Johnny."

Johnny went outside and began to walk. "Walk, walk, walk," he said. "I'm getting tired of all this walking."

Suddenly he saw something shiny on the sidewalk. "What's this?" he said. "It's money right here on the sidewalk! Now I can run to the ice cream store."

So Johnny ran to the ice cream store.

"Boy, what a great place!" he said. "Just look at all the different kinds of ice cream. There are so many kinds that I don't know which one to pick."

"Take your time," said the man.

"The chocolate looks good," said Johnny at last. "I would like a chocolate ice cream cone."

Johnny ate his ice cream cone
on the way home.

"Mother!" said Johnny. "Guess what I found on my walk this time. I found money! I found money and I got an ice cream cone."

"You did?" said Mother. "The money was a good find, wasn't it?"

The next morning Johnny did all the same things. He ate breakfast. He made his bed. He cleaned up his room.

After that Johnny went to his mother and said, "Mother, I am going for a walk."

His mother said, "Have a good time, Johnny."

Johnny walked and walked and walked.
He walked up and down. He walked
around and around.

Suddenly Johnny saw a little puppy in the
street. "Here, puppy. Here, puppy," he called.

But the puppy did not move out of the street.

Johnny looked both ways for cars. Then he ran to get the puppy out of the street.

"Oh, you poor little thing," said Johnny. "Don't you have a home? You must be lost. I'll bet you need something to eat. Do you want to come home with me? Maybe I can keep you."

Johnny took the puppy home.

"Mother!" said Johnny. "Look what I found on my walk this time. She is so little. I think she is lost. May we keep her, Mother?"

"Well," said Mother. "First let's read the Lost and Found part of the newspaper."

Mother looked in the newspaper. "No, I don't see anything about a lost puppy in here," she said. "Now we will make some signs."

Johnny and his mother made signs. The signs looked like this.

They put one sign on a tree. They put another sign in the ice cream store. When they got home, the telephone rang.

"I see you found my puppy," said a man on the telephone. "You can have her. I can't take care of her."

Mother told Johnny what the man had said. "You can keep the puppy, Johnny," said Mother. "She's as cute as a button."

"Cute as a button. Cute as a button," said Johnny. "Oh, Mother. Button would be a nice name for her."

Then Johnny called to the puppy. "Here, Button. Here, Button. Now you are my puppy. We'll be such good friends."

Every morning after that, Johnny got up
early and ate a good breakfast. Then he
made his bed, cleaned up his room, and
went for a walk with Button.

And sometimes Mother went
walking with them.

READING REINFORCEMENT

The following activities support the findings of the National Reading Panel that determined the most effective components for reading instruction are: Phonemic Awareness, Phonics, Vocabulary, Fluency, and Text Comprehension.

Phonemic Awareness: The long /ī/ sound

Sound Substitution: Say the words on the left to your child. Ask your child to repeat the word, changing the short /i/ sound to a long /ī/ sound:

lick=like	hid=hide	bit=bite	mill=mile	lit=light
fit=fight	kit=kite	sit=sight	fin=fine	dim=dime
pick=pike	rip=ripe	Tim=time	knit=knight	

Phonics: The long /ī/ spelling

1. Make four columns on a blank sheet of paper and label each with the spellings for long /ī/: i_e, ie, igh, y

2. Write the following words on separate index cards:

bike	pie	high	sky	shine	tries
tie	my	rice	right	fly	try
cry	cries	side	night	ice	might
fries	fry	rid	bright	time	

3. Ask your child to read each word and place the card under the column heading that represents the long /ī/ spelling in the word.

Vocabulary: Verb Tenses

1. Write each of the following words on separate index cards:

walk/walking/walked   eat/eating/ate
sleep/sleeping/slept   read/reading/read
write/writing/wrote   jump/jumping/jumped
hide/hiding/hid   help/helping/helped
play/playing/played   find/finding/found

30

2. Mix up the index cards and ask your child to group them in verb families. Ask your child to place the verbs in each family according to tense (present, present + ing, past) and read them aloud in order.

3. Put the cards in a paper bag and shake it to mix them up. Take turns selecting cards from the bag and stating sentences using the words.

Fluency: Shared Reading

1. Reread the story with your child at least two more times while your child tracks the print by running a finger under the words as they are read. Ask your child to read the words he or she knows with you.

2. Reread the story, stopping occasionally so your child can supply the next word without looking. For example, *During the school year Johnny got up early every* _____ (morning).

3. Have your child reread the story, stopping occasionally for you to supply the next word.

Text Comprehension: Discussion Time

1. Ask your child to retell the sequence of events in the story.

2. To check comprehension, ask your child the following questions:

   • What did Johnny do each morning during the school year?

   • Why did Johnny's mother keep telling him to take a walk?

   • Why do you think Johnny stopped saying there wasn't anything to do?

   • Why did Johnny's mother look in the newspaper and help him make signs?

   • Have you ever found anything while taking a walk? What do you think you might find in your neighborhood?

WORD LIST

In addition to giving practice with words that most children will recognize, **Take a Walk, Johnny** uses the 35 enrichment words listed below.

breakfast	mirror	telephone
bridges		tired
bumps	nice	toad
butterfly		
button	outside	wonder
		wonderful
chocolate	plants	
circuses	poor	
cone		
cowboys	rang	
cream	rock(s)	
cute		
	shine	
dressed	shiny	
during	sidewalk	
	signs	
early	spots	
elephants	suddenly	
ice		
idea		

ABOUT THE AUTHOR Margaret Hillert has written over 80 books for children who are just learning to read. Her books have been translated into many different languages and over a million children throughout the world have read her books. She first started writing poetry as a child and has continued to write for children and adults throughout her life. A first grade teacher for 34 years, Margaret is now retired from teaching and lives in Michigan where she likes to write, take walks in the morning, and care for her three cats.

Photograph by Glenna Washburn

ABOUT THE ADVISER Shannon Cannon contributed the activities pages that appear in this book. Shannon serves as a literacy consultant and provides staff development to help improve reading instruction. She is a frequent presenter at educational conferences and workshops. Prior to this she worked as an elementary school teacher and as president of a curriculum publishing company.